Hiking Trip to bring:

- [ ] Hiking Boots
- [ ] Sun Screen ☀
- [ ] bug spray
- [ ] Binoculars
- [ ] goggles
- [ ] flippers
- [ ] water bottles 💧
- [ ] flashlight
- [ ] band-aids (just in case)
- [ ] Snacks

Animals to look for:

- [ ] Blue Jay
- [ ] Cardinal
- [ ] woodpecker
- [ ] ducks
- [ ] owl (at night)

- [ ] Frog
- [ ] turtle
- [ ] fish
- [ ] snail

- [ ] Inchworm
- [ ] Ladybug
- [ ] dragonfly
- [ ] Spider
- [ ] fireflies (at night)

Quack

GROCERIES

PEANUT BUTTER
BREAD
APPLES → Choc...

Yes, Let's

By Galen Goodwin Longstreth

Illustrated by Maris Wicks

Published by Tanglewood Publishing, Inc., April, 2013
© 2013 Galen Goodwin Longstreth and Maris Wicks

Design by Amy Alick Perich

Tanglewood Publishing, Inc.
4400 Hulman St.
Terre Haute, IN 47803
www.tanglewoodbooks.com

Printed in Illinois, U.S.A.
10 9 8 7 6 5 4 3 2

ISBN 1-933718-87-0
ISBN 978-1-933718-87-3

54135917   07/14

Library of Congress Cataloging-in-Publication Data

Longstreth, Galen Goodwin.
  Yes, let's / by Galen Goodwin Longstreth ; illustrated by Maris Wicks.
      pages cm.
  Summary: Relates, through illustrations and simple, rhyming text, a family's day in the woods, including a hike, swimming, and a picnic.
  ISBN-13: 978-1-933718-87-3 (hardback)
  ISBN-10: 1-933718-87-0
  [1. Stories in rhyme. 2. Family life--Fiction. 3. Outdoor life--Fiction.] I. Title.
  PZ8.3.L8612Yes 2013
  [E]--dc23
                        2012045312

Dedication

For Greg

–G.L. & M.W.

Let's wake up extra early,

before the day gets hot.

Let's pack a picnic, hurry up—ready or not.

Let's get into the station wagon,
roll those windows down.

Let's sing out loud and wave to cows
as we drive out of town.

Let's park the car beneath the trees
and trade our shoes for boots.

Let's hike the trail, hop the stream,
and duck the fallen logs.

Let's go this way, we've got all day—
someone call the dog.

Let's shed our packs and clothes and caps and race down to the river.

Let's jump and splash and dive and slide
and tumble in the water.

Let's hold our breath, turn somersaults,
catch minnows in our hands.

Let's share the fins and goggles,
look for treasure in the sand.

Let's gather rocks and build a dam
and make a little boat.

Let's try with leaves and bark and grass
until it finally floats.

Let's scramble up the riverbank
when it is time for lunch.

Let's feast on tasty picnic treats,
gimmee—gobble—crunch!

Let's find out what's beyond that stump,
but let's not go too far.

Let's choose a stone to bring back home,
or maybe this huge spider.

Let's lace our boots and pack our trash,
now all our bags are lighter.

Let's find the path, don't be last,
our shadows lead the way.

Let's tend to bugbites, aches, and scrapes, strike a tired pose.

Let's load the car and pile in,
it's time to head for home.

Let's stop for dinner on the way, milkshakes all around.

Let's fall asleep as stars come out,
no one makes a sound.

Let's climb the stairs and into bed,
now that the sun has set.

And dream of going back again,
another day...